W9-BYK-196

Monkey: Not Ready for Bedtime

Marc Brown

Alfred A. Knopf · New York

But Monkey couldn't fall asleep.

Mommy warms up some milk.

Mr. Fuzzy tries to help.

Daddy gives
Monkey
a backrub.

But every night
it's the same problem.
Monkey is just **not**
ready for bed.

It's no fun
being tired at school.

But then Monkey's brother has an idea.

"Some people count things to fall asleep. Find something you really like and count it slowly."

That night, Monkey tries
counting bugs.

Red crayons.

Toys.

Raspberry ice cream
cones.

But it wasn't
working.

Two Iguanodons.

Three Triceratops...

This was fun.

He flies with the Dimorphodons.

He rocks with T.rex.

All the dinosaurs join in. It's a dinosaur jamboree.

He Scoots down a Diplodocus.

He races with the Gallimimus.

And before long,
it's no surprise
that they all get
very, very, very sleepy.

Monkey, too.

·For·

·Jenny and Isabel·

THIS IS A BORZOI BOOK PUBLISHED BY ALFRED A. KNOPF

Copyright © 2017 by Marc Brown

All rights reserved. Published in the United States by Alfred A. Knopf, an imprint of Random House Children's Books, a division of Penguin Random House LLC, New York.

Knopf, Borzoi Books, and the colophon are registered trademarks of Penguin Random House LLC.

Visit us on the Web! randomhousekids.com

Educators and librarians, for a variety of teaching tools, visit us at RHTeachersLibrarians.com

Library of Congress Cataloging-in-Publication Data is available upon request.
ISBN 978-1-101-93761-7 (trade) — ISBN 978-1-101-93762-4 (lib. bdg.) —
ISBN 978-1-101-93763-1 (ebook)

The text of this book was created by hand by Marc Brown, accompanied by a few typeset bits in Elephant.
The illustrations were created using colored pencils and gouache.

MANUFACTURED IN CHINA
September 2017
10 9 8 7 6 5 4 3 2 1
First Edition

Random House Children's Books supports the First Amendment and celebrates the right to read.